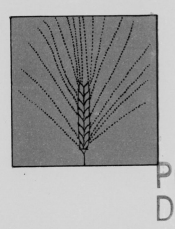
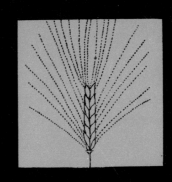

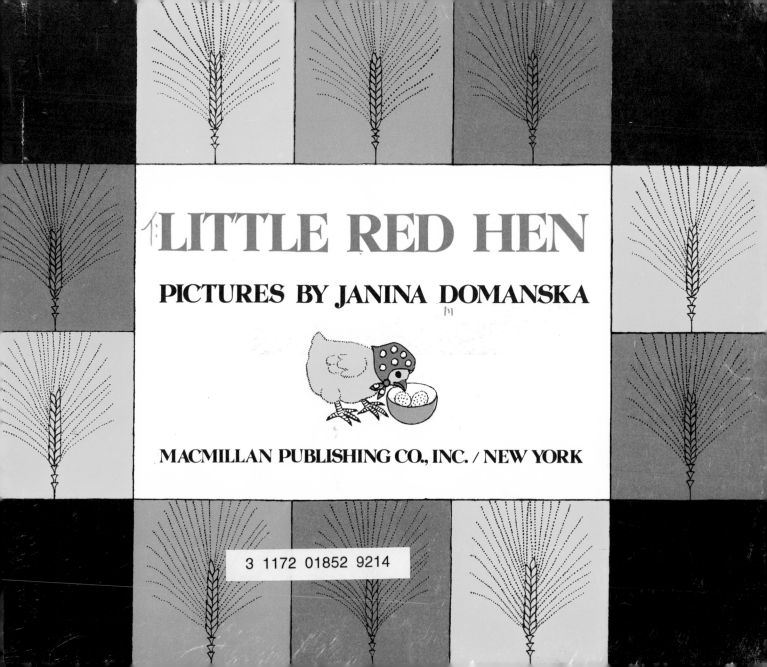

LITTLE RED HEN

PICTURES BY JANINA DOMANSKA

MACMILLAN PUBLISHING CO., INC. / NEW YORK

Macmillan Publishing Co., Inc., 866 Third Avenue, New York, N.Y. 10022. Collier-Macmillan Canada Ltd., Toronto, Ontario. Library of Congress catalog card number: 72-92436. Printed in the United States of America. 1 2 3 4 5 6 7 8 9 10

Library of Congress Cataloging in Publication Data
Little red hen. Little red hen. [1. Folklore] I. Domanska, Janina, illus
II. Title. PZ8.1.L72Do 398.2'452 [E] 72-92436 ISBN 0-02-732820-

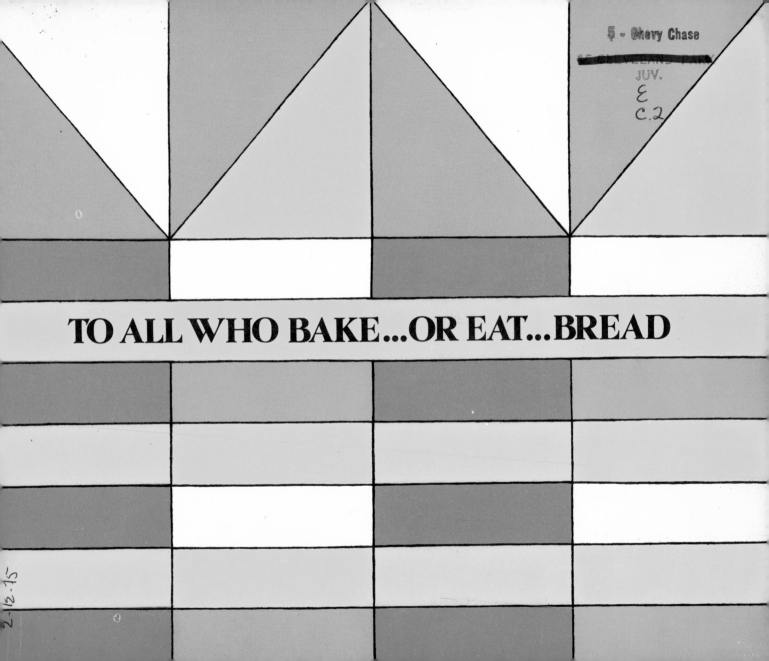

TO ALL WHO BAKE...OR EAT...BREAD

Little Red Hen found a grain of wheat.

"Who will plant this?" she asked.
"Not I," said the cat.
"Not I," said the goose.
"Not I," said the rat.
"Then I will," said Little Red Hen.

So she buried the wheat in the ground.

After a while it grew up yellow and ripe.

"The wheat is ripe now," said Little Red Hen.
"Who will cut and thresh it?"
"Not I," said the cat.
"Not I," said the goose.
"Not I," said the rat.
"Then I will,"
  said Little Red Hen.

So she cut it with her bill

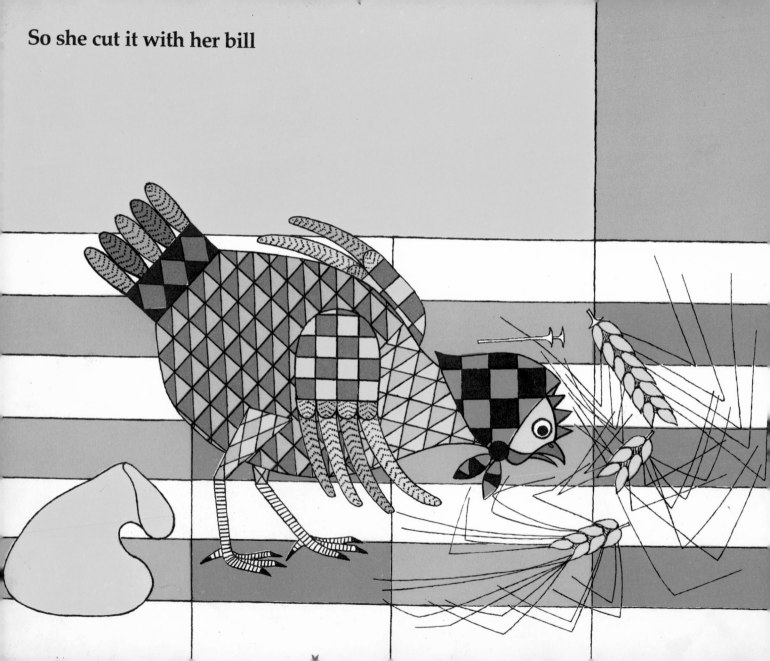

and threshed it with her wings.

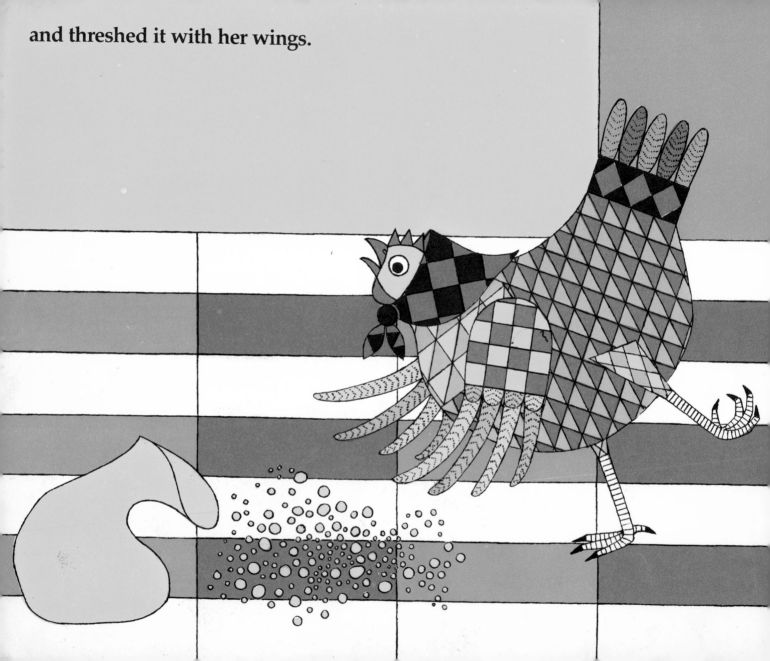

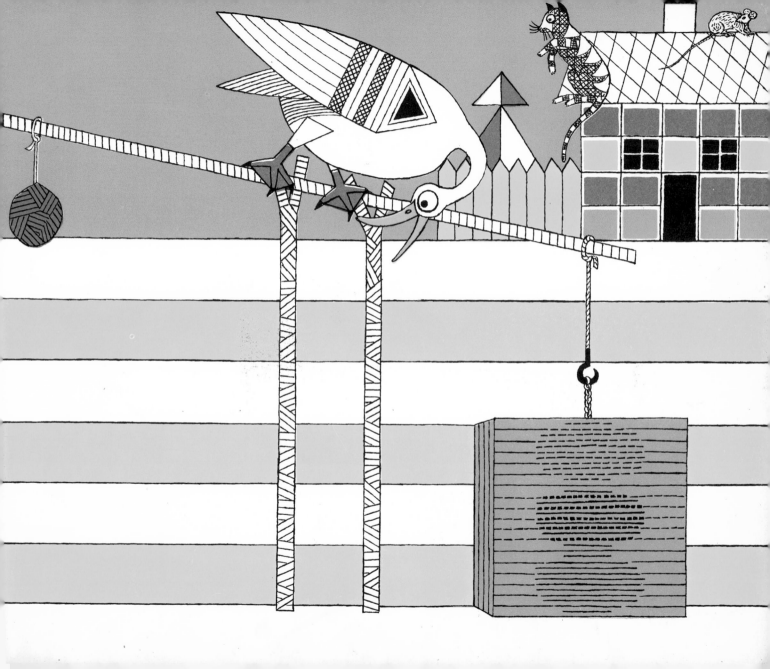

Then she asked, "Who will take
this wheat to the mill?"
"Not I," said the cat.
"Not I," said the goose.
"Not I," said the rat.
"Then I will," said Little Red Hen.

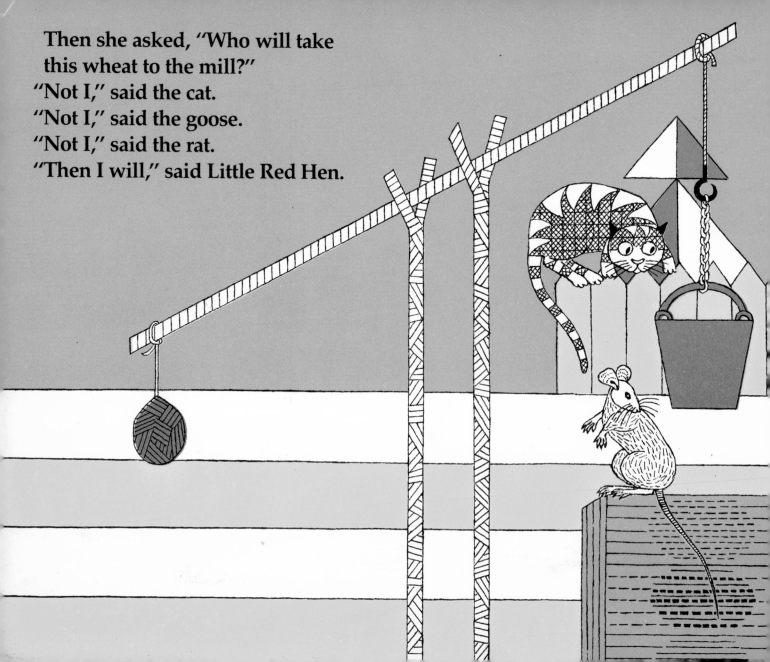

So she carried the wheat to the mill,
where it was ground.

Then she carried the flour home.

"Who will make me some bread
 with this flour?" she asked.
"Not I," said the cat.
"Not I," said the goose.
"Not I," said the rat.
"Then I will,"
 said Little Red Hen.

So she made the bread and baked it.

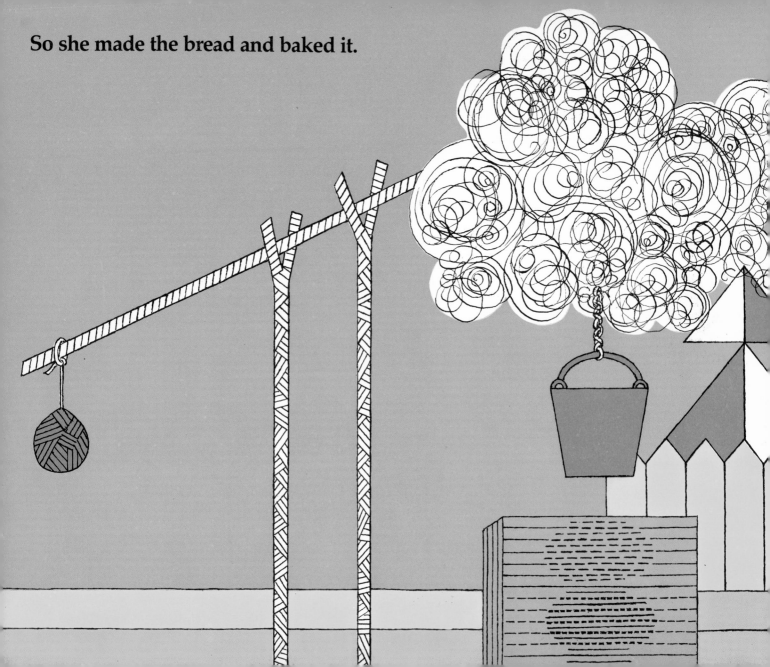

Then she said, "Now we shall see
who will eat this bread."
"I will," said the cat.
"I will," said the goose.
"I will," said the rat.
"I am quite sure you would,"
  said Little Red Hen,
"if you could get it."

Then she called her chicks,

and they ate up all the bread.
There was none left
for the cat,
or the goose,
or the rat.